CHICKEN JOE FORGETS SOMETHING IMPORTANT

STORY AND SONGS BY
TROUT FISHING IN AMERICA
ILLUSTRATED BY STÉPHANE JORISCH

It was a quiet and peaceful morning on the farm.
Almost all of the animals were still sleeping.

Chicken Joe, the cat who slept in the hen house, was smiling and having a wonderful dream about playing his favorite electric guitar.

"Rock and Roll! Rock and Roll! Rock and Roll!"

Chicken Joe opened one eye. Why do roosters wake up so early? Why are they yelling 'Rock and Roll' before breakfast? Don't they realize a cat needs sixteen or seventeen hours of sleep every day?

He wanted to go back to his dream, but he was awake now. There was something important about today that he needed to remember, but he was still sleepy and he forgot what it was.

He decided to make the best of a bad start and he climbed out of bed.

- "Good morning," yawned Chicken Joe. "How are those eggs doing?"

- "Very well," clucked Hilda proudly. "We put them all in one basket and all ten of them will hatch tomorrow."

- "That's wonderful, what are you hens up to today?"

- "We're going to help bake a cake!" cackled Helen.

- "Really? What kind of cake?"

- "That's for me to know and you to find out," replied Helen.

- "How are you today, Chicken Joe?" asked Hilda, quickly changing the subject.

- "Not bad, but I forgot something important when I woke up."

Helen and Hilda knew exactly what he had forgotten.

– "You probably forgot about the big game," said Helen.

– "Is there a big game coming up?"

– "No, there isn't," laughed Hilda.

– "She just said that because she thought it might help you remember."

That didn't make any sense at all to Chicken Joe and he couldn't figure out why these silly hens were giggling. He nodded sleepily and headed outside.

– "Its time for breakfast. I forget some things but I never forget to eat."

Chicken Joe made his way through the pines toward the farmhouse. He saw his best friend, a city dog named Miss Kitty who was spending the summer on the farm. She was a little dog, but she was pulling a big red wagon full of stuff.

- "What do you have in there?"

- "Oh, nothing much. A few newspapers, a pound of flour, a bit of salt, some strings, two bags of candy, and some paint."

- "What for?"

- "That's for me to know and you to find out," she answered playfully and quickly changed the subject. "How are you today, Chicken Joe?"

- "Not bad, but I forgot something important when I woke up."

- "Maybe you forgot your homework. Tell the teacher I ate it. I'm sure she'll believe you."

- "I don't even go to school," laughed Chicken Joe as he turned towards the farmhouse. "Anyway, I'm going to get some breakfast. I forget some things but I never forget to eat."

As Chicken Joe came out from the forest, he saw Mister, a very smart but very strange mule. Mister was playing a kazoo like a party animal.

- "What nonsense are you up to, Mister?"

- "I need to sneeze and I'd rather play the kazoo at you than say achoo at you," answered the mule playfully. He quickly changed the subject. "How are you today, Chicken Joe?"

- "Not bad, but I forgot something important when I woke up."

- Mister looked very serious and said, "I've found the best way to remember something is to sing backwards. Forgotten things pop right into your brain. Or mumble a silly sentence like 'The fish swim backwards in the sky'. That works, too."

- "I'll try that later. Right now I'm getting hungry. I forget some things but I never forget to eat."

Chicken Joe pushed through the pet door into the farmhouse. As he entered, he knew something was wrong. His food bowl was empty and the house was totally silent. He couldn't even hear King Kong, the noisy parakeet that always complained about Mr. Fred's fiddle playing and Ms. Naomi's yodeling.

Had everyone left and forgotten to bring him along?

Chicken Joe checked every room in the house. Nobody was home. Where did everybody go? He sat down on the pillow Ms. Naomi knitted for him when he was just a kitten. This was turning out to be a bad day. First, he had forgotten something important and now he was sad, hungry, and all alone. He licked his paws for a bit and hummed a song backwards, like Mister had suggested. Then he fell asleep.

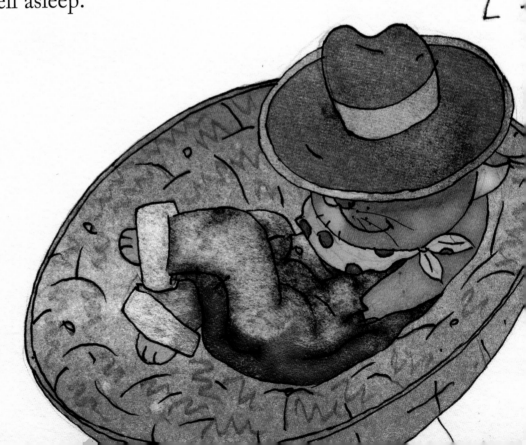

An hour or so later, Chicken Joe woke
to the sound of singing voices and a blast
from an electric guitar. He jumped up on
the counter so he could see out
the kitchen window.

He saw a fish piñata hanging from the giant oak tree. On the table nearby, he spotted a chocolate cake and some pretty packages. Helen, Hilda, Miss Kitty, Mister, King Kong, Mr. Fred, Ms. Naomi, and even the Rock and Roll Roosters... all of his friends were there making music and laughing about how cats can sleep all day.

The backwards phrase - Birthday Happy - popped right into his brain and suddenly Chicken Joe remembered. Today was his birthday.

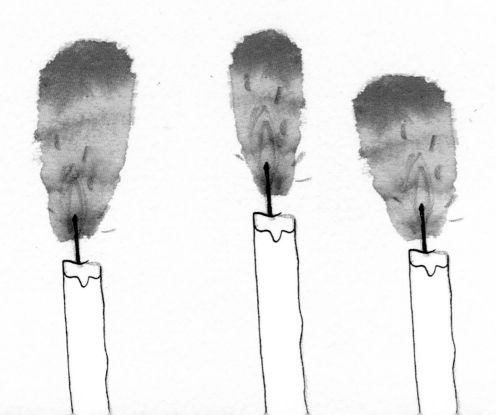

Rock and Roll Roosters

Some folks like to rock and roll
When the sun goes down
They get ready to party, all dressed up
Get out and paint the town
When it gets dark we count sheep
Close our eyes and just go to sleep
Cause when the sun comes up
That's when we get down

Yeah, in the morning light
We like to strut our stuff
We're Rock and Roll Roosters
And we never get enough
Flap our wings, dance around
Rock the world with a mighty sound
Yeah, when the sun comes up
That's when we get down

Listen to us sing, we go like this
Rock and roll, rock and roll, rock and roll!
Rock and roll, rock and roll, rock and roll!
Flap our wings, puff up proud
Take a deep breath and scream right out loud
Rock and roll, rock and roll, rock and roll!

Lazy cats lay around
They like to sleep all day.
Rock and Roll Roosters gotta to get things done
We don't have time to waste
Flap our wings, dance around
Rock the world with a mighty sound
When the sun comes up
That's when we get down

We go just like this, we say,
Rock and roll, rock and roll, rock and roll!
Rock and roll, rock and roll, rock and roll!
Flap our wings, puff up proud
Take a deep breath and scream right out loud
Rock and roll, rock and roll, rock and roll!

16 or 17 Hours of Sleep

I need 16 or 17 hours of sleep
At least 16 hours of sleep
To have a good day, I've got to say
I had 16 hours of way down deep
16 or 17 hours of sleep
At least 16 hours of sleep
On a feather bed I'm going to lay my head
And get 16 or 17 hours of sleep

1 hour – That's feeling fine
2 hours – It's a really good time
3 hours - Don't wake me up
There's not enough coffee in a coffee cup
4 hours - I'm picking up steam
5 hours - Starting to dream
But 6 got scared 'cause 7 ate 9
I love that joke so I used that line

10 hours – That's better than none
11 hours - I'm getting it done
12 and 13 and 14, too
My eyes won't open they're stuck like glue
15 hours – That's baby stuff
15 and a half - Still not enough
16 or 17 hours for me
I'd sleep longer but I've got to eat!

Hello, My Chicken Thinks He's a Dog

The chicken ate my homework
It wasn't my fault
That psycho chicken thinks that he's a dog
Buck, buck, barks at the mailman, always chasing cats
Ate so many dog biscuits that chicken's getting fat
Digs in the garbage, races after cars
Tried to walk him on a leash, we didn't get too far

He followed me to school
It wasn't my fault
That psycho chicken thinks that he's a dog
Buck, buck, barks at strangers and people on their bikes
Tried to feed him chicken scratch but that's not what he likes
He howls at the moon with the bad dogs every night
When the sun comes up he just won't act right

The chicken likes fireplugs
It isn't my fault
That psycho chicken thinks that he's a dog
Buck, buck, barks at everything from morning until night
We take him to a dog park but he just wants to fight
Got a T-shirt that says, "Big Dog", really likes to fetch
Tried to teach him to roll over but he hasn't learned that yet

Through the Pines

The summer breeze smells like Christmas trees
My shoes smell bad as turpentine
When I'm walking there I can float in the air
On that little ol' path through the pines
Now I've been told there are streets of gold
Oh how they sparkle and they shine, shine, shine
But they can't compete when I set my feet
On that little old path through the pines

Through the pines
That little old path through the pines
No they can't compete when I set my feet
On that little old path through the pines

The man in the moon is a big balloon
Rising on the ridge at suppertime
Whistle and smile I'll be there in a while
On that little old path through the pines

Through the pines
That little old path through the pines
Whistle and smile I'll be there in a while
On that little old path through the pines

Katie kissed a frog that was sitting on a log
Hoping for a handsome prince to find
But her hair turned green and
the frog began to scream
On that little old path through the pines

Through the pines
That little old path through the pines
But her hair turned green and
the frog began to scream
On that little old path through the pines
Whistle and smile, I'll be there in a while
On that little old path through the pines

For Me to Know and You to Find Out

Whatcha gonna do?
Where you gonna go?
How you gonna get there?
Whatcha gonna take?
When's it gonna start?
Should I bring an arm chair?
Hold on, stop jackin' your jaw
Talk so much you make me want to shout
Don't want to hurt your feelings but all I can say
Is that's for me to know and you to find out

How's it gonna happen?
Where's it gonna be?
Does it cost to get inside?
What should I wear?
Is it gonna be a party?
Porterhouse or chicken fried?
Hold on, stop jackin' your jaw
Talk so much you make me want to shout
Don't want to hurt your feelings but all I can say
Is that's for me to know and you to find out

That's for me to know and you to find out
Me to know and you to find out
That's for me to know and you to find out
I ain't playing, I'm just saying
Way beyond a shadow of a doubt
Don't want to hurt your feelings but all I can say
Is that's for me to know and you to find out

Is it bigger than a breadbox?
Smaller than a house?
Animal or vegetable?
Have I seen it in a movie?
Is it on the TV?
Or classified a mineral?
Hold on, stop jacking your jaw
Talk so much you make me want to shout
Don't want to hurt your feelings but all I can say
Is that's for me to know and you to find out

Where you gonna go with two bags of candy?
Why you got a paint can?
Whatcha gonna do with all that newspaper?
Whatcha gonna make man?
Hold on, stop jacking your jaw
Talk so much you make me want to shout
Don't want to hurt your feelings but all I can say
Is that's for me to know and you to find out

The Fish Swim Backwards in the Sky

It's a fine, fine day and a fine day it is
It's a good thing cows can't fly
It's a fine, fine day and a fine day it is
The fish swim backwards in the sky
Yes, the fish are swimming backwards in the sky

Roll on the rollers, skate on the skates
A kiss on the kisser, a date for the dates
Hum-de-dum-dum, dum-de-doh-doh
Barefoot dancing in the snow
The bear does a foot dance in the snow

Good afternoon, after noon it is
What's good about goodbye?
Good afternoon, after noon it is
The fish swim backwards in the sky
Yes, the fish are swimming backwards in the sky

Over here I overheard
First comes second then comes third
Hum-de-dum-dum, dum-de-doh-dee
Don't hold hands with a cactus tree
Don't hold hands with a cactus tree

It's a quiet night and a quiet night it is
Shadows are stealing the light
It's a quiet night and a quiet night it is
The fish swim backwards in the sky
Yes, the fish are swimming backwards in the sky

C-A-T in the H-E-N House

There's a C-A-T in the H-E-N house
What's that cat doing there?
A C-A-T with the H-E-Ns
Those silly hens don't really care

There's a D-O-G in the D-O-G house
Wants a W-A-L-K
Dogs go C-R-A-Z-Y
If that word you ever say

If you can S-P-E-L-L it out
You'll know what they're spelling about
Let me spell you something true
I L-O-V-E-Y-O-U

There's a B-I-R-D in a birdhouse
He's a handsome parakeet
Put your finger in his cage
You'll find out he's not too sweet
There's an F-R-O-G on a lily pad
He sounds so sad
Singing songs that hurt so bad
Frog karaoke on a lily pad

There's an M-U-L-E singing opera
But he sounds a little hoarse
He's not an H-O-R-S-E
He's a mule without a voice
There's a P-I-G in the bathroom
I've really, really gotta go
What's that pig doing in the bathroom?
I don't think I want to know

Where Did Everybody Go?

I was running with a fast crowd
Then I tried to take it slow
Closed my eyes, turned around
Where did everybody go?
I was just laughing with my friends
Now I'm feeling so low
Closed my eyes, turned around
Where did everybody go?

I know it's not forever
It's not the end of the world
Right now all I need to know
Is where did everybody go?

Did I go and make a wrong turn?
Miss a sign along the road?
Closed my eyes, turned around
Where did everybody go?
Crossed a busy street all by myself
Left without a hand to hold
Closed my eyes, turned around
Where did everybody go?

You've Got a Funny Name

Hey Chicken Joe, where did you go?
It's cold and it's time to go to bed
If you won't come inside
You'll have to spend the night outside
Did you hear what I said?
You'll be sleeping with the chickens
What do you think about that?
Hey Chicken Joe
You've got a funny name for a cat

Here Kitty, Kitty won't you come back home
So Chicken Joe won't be alone?
You've been playing all day
With the dogs down the lane
Chewing on an old neck bone
You've been rollin' in the pasture
Sleeping in a log
Hey Miss Kitty
You've got a funny name for a dog

Hey King Kong
Won't you sing me a song?
You're sitting in a corner in your cage
You chirp and you chatter
When the sun comes up
But never have a single thing to say
It's a running conversation
But you never say a word
Hey King Kong
You've got a funny name for a bird

Nice to meet you, Mister
I don't want to shake your hand
It sounds rude but I know you understand
You've been sitting in the shade
Thinking you've got it made
Spitting in an old tin can
You seem pretty smart
But you never went to school
Hey there Mister
You've got a funny name for a mule

The Big Game

Everybody's getting ready
Everybody's getting set
The clock is tick-tocking but it's not time yet
We've been waiting all year
Wound up all week
We're so excited we can barely speak

Here it comes!
It's the Big Game!
The big, big, Big Game
The biggest game on the biggest stage
Packed with all the biggest names
Rocking and rolling, we're going insane
It's the Big Game
Really, really, really Big Game

They're focusing the spotlight, popping up the corn
Banging on the drum and blaring on the horn
Hearts are going thumpidy-thump
We're jumping up and down
Who's going to be there?
Everyone in town

Flags are flying in the breeze
Banners are waving in the sky
If our team wins
We're going to celebrate
But if we lose we'll try not to cry

Dance With Me

The hands on the wall barely move at all
When I'm waiting to be with you
But time slips away whenever we go out and play
And I can't seem to hold on tight enough

Then I look out the window and what do I see?
But my friends, they're all smiling at me
So I hold out my hand, ask if you'd like to dance
And smile for a while, dance with me
Dansez avec moi, gentille fille

My friends are here with me in a land of make-believe
And it's real enough to hold all our dreams
So I hold out my hand, ask if you'd like to dance
And smile for a while, dance with me
Dansez avec moi, gentille fille

Story and songs by Trout Fishing in America (Ezra Idlet and Keith Grimwood)
Record Producers Ezra Idlet and Keith Grimwood Artistic Director Roland Stringer
Illustrator Stephane Jorisch Design Stephan Lorti for Haus Design
Narration Keith Grimwood and Ezra Idlet

Lead vocals

Keith Grimwood The Big Game, Rock and Roll Roosters, For Me to Know and You to Find Out,
C-A-T in the H-E-N House, 16 or 17 Hours of Sleep
Ezra Idlet You've Got a Funny Name, Where Did Everybody Go?, Through the Pines,
The Fish Swim Backwards in the Sky, Hello, My Chicken Thinks He's a Dog, Dance With Me

Musicians

Keith Grimwood string bass, bass guitar, synthesizer, hand claps, harmony vocals
Ezra Idlet guitar, banjo, mandolin, spoons, bouzouki, percussion, hand claps, harmony vocals
Jeneé Fleenor violin (Where Did Everybody Go?, Through the Pines, The Fish Swim Backwarpds
in the Sky, C-A-T in the H-E-N House) Terrance Simien accordian (Dance with me)
Ralph Fontenot frottoir / rub-board (Dance with me) Kim Deschamps lap steel (The Big Game)
Fred Bogert piano (For Me to Know and You to Find Out)

The song Hello, My Chicken Thinks He's a Dog was written during a workshop with
6th Graders at Cook Elementary, Ft. Smith, AR that happened on February 21, 2008

Special thanks to Karen Thom, Dick Renko, Suzanne Renko,
Beth Grimwood, Kathy O'Connell, Kenny, Mindy and Robbie

Artist information available at www.troutmusic.com
Also by Trout Fishing in America My Name is Chicken Joe (9782923163499)
Master recordings under license from Trout Fishing in America
All songs published by Troutoons Ⓟ 2010

Ⓟ www.thesecretmountain.com
ⒸⓅ 2011 The Secret Mountain (Folle Avoine Productions)
ISBN-10 2-923163-74-5 / ISBN-13 978-2-923163-74-1